Death and the Detective

A Word Prompt-inspired Series

Cathy Miller

Old Lady Biz Publishing

ISBN - Paperback: ISBN: 979-8-9933529-3-0

ISBN – ePub: 979-8-9933529-2-3

Book Cover by Bryce Kmetz

Dedicated to my online friend and Master Originator of the word prompt site, Creative Copy Challenge (CCC), Shane Arthur.

And to all the talented creators I had the pleasure of meeting at CCC. Your encouragement and support prompted the dream to publication. And for that, I am eternally grateful.

Contents

Introduction

BACK IN 2009, I had been freelancing as a business writer for only a year. My boomer brain does not remember how, but I stumbled across a site, Creative Copy Challenge.

The brainchild of super editor, Shane Arthur, Creative Copy Challenge (CCC) was one of my happiest discoveries. The concept was simple. CCC posted 10 random words or phrases. It invited writers and non-writers to use the 10 words/phrases "in a creative, cohesive short story."

Shane moved on from the site, but one of its longtime contributors, Kathleen MK, kept it going for years but the site moved to Facebook. Unfortunately, I do not know its current location.

Like several contributors back then, I developed a series with some of the posted words. My series became known as Death and the Detective. I decided to collect the entries and put them in this book. Entries are in their original state with minor editing for spelling and other written oops. Sometimes I used the word prompts in another form other than the detective series, which is why the Challenge numbers do not always follow sequentially.

The words you see in **BOLD** are the challenge words. Some of the word prompts became even more challenging. Included are definitions of the more obscure ones.

I hope you enjoy the read. Who knows. Maybe I'll create a real series.

Take the Challenge

Note: if you would like to try out some word prompts, I have included some sites that offer word prompts at the end of this book. I have also listed the word prompts for the Challenges used in this series.

Challenge #1

Oops - I Did

It's hard to say what makes a good detective – especially a homicide one. What is that **x-factor** that gets a detective up every morning, especially after all he has seen? How is it he still finds a purpose for life?

Brett Connors had been a homicide detective for 25 years. It stopped being a job years ago – it simply was his life, who he was. It was mornings like this when he had to reach deep to find that purpose for life. The killing of a child never made sense. Why should he go on when one so small, so innocent, could not.

The trial was this morning. The courthouse sat next to the **townhall**, its shadows reflecting Brett's own dark mood. Like most cops, Brett hated testifying – not that he didn't want to nail the son of a bitch. No, it was the frustration from the many times the system made a mockery of what he called justice.

Settling in a seat at the back of the courtroom, Brett barely registered the **parrot** repetition of the bailiff's instructions. His mind replayed the tragic scene as if he was standing there now, instead of all those months ago.

He saw it all – the silky, blonde hair, stiffened by blood, like the small body robbed of life – the baby smooth skin, drained of the innocence of youth. Why couldn't he be at some ball game, with a glove on one hand, and a box of **Cracker Jacks** in the other? That's what the life of a 7-year-old boy should be – not this caricature of evil. There should never be **unions** made of children and death.

As the crime scene technicians gathered evidence, Brett walked over to the computer sitting on a child's desk. Shifting the mouse, Brett brought the monitor to life. If only he could do the same for a small boy. That is when he saw it – **Google**, shouting beneath its rainbow hue, THOU SHALT NOT KILL – OOPS – I DID.

It was all Brett could do to stop from smashing a fist through the vile words. At least when he touched the mouse, he used the sadly ironic birthday **napkins** lying on the desk – not that he expected prints. Brett prayed there really was a God, one that would banish the killer to eternal hell. He had no doubt he violated more than one of **the 10 Commandments**.

"All rise for the Honorable Judge James Angel."

Pulled back to the present, Brett wondered if his thoughts of God had sent him Judge Angel. God, he hoped so. The city of **San Francisco** could use some divine help – otherwise, it was going to be a long, **cold season** of killing.

Challenge #2

Erase the Horror

"FINALLY, A WIN FOR the good guys," Brett mused.

There was little satisfaction, however, hearing the "Guilty" conviction. No amount of the killer's suffering could erase the horror of a murdered child, one not far removed from **Winnie the Pooh** tales and the Tooth Fairy.

You would think with a **prior work history** spanning 25 years as a homicide detective, Brett's hardened heart would not ache quite so much. But a cop, unshaken by the death of a child, had better turn in his badge.

A weary, lined face stared back from the **bathroom** mirror. Lack of sleep and eyes that saw too much did that. Try as he might to shut it out, the **song** kept playing over and over in his head.

Well, You know you make me want to shout
Kick my heals up and shout
Throw my hands up and shout
Throw my head back and shout[1]

He had no idea what put it in his head. All he knew was that he wanted to do a whole lot more than shout. A **head-shot** blast aimed at the killer had a much better ring to it. But, then the **authorities** frowned on that kind of thing, especially in today's world of **lawsuits**, targeted at those who serve and protect.

Those who pushed the **propaganda** that all cops were heartless bastards never saw the things that Brett had. If they experienced even a third of what he had, they might recognize his hard exterior as the defense mechanism against a crippling world of hurt.

Stepping into the shower, Brett let the cold, hard spray reduce the song to the distant **twitter** of sound. Routine was his salvation – a cold shower, a hit of **orange juice**, and he was ready to face another day.

---

1. The Isley Brothers, "Shout - Part 1 & 2," recorded July 29, 1959, RCA Victor 47-7588, 1959, 7-inch single

Challenge #3
Sawubona

Brett Connors had been a homicide detective for 25 years. He couldn't remember doing anything else, and he couldn't remember the last time he had a day off.

His lieutenant had given him no choice – take the week off or cover the precinct's front desk for the scheduled school tours.

Although he resisted, Brett decided to get the hell out of Dodge – or more accurately, San Francisco. He hopped on a plane and found himself sitting on a beach in Encinitas, California. Located in the north county of San Diego, Brett considered it as one of the few true beach towns left in southern California.

"**Sawubona**," came the whispered voice.

Looking up from a book he wasn't really reading, Brett responded, "Excuse me?"

"Sawubona. It is from my native Zulu language." Her accent was slight, but her beauty knew no bounds. Standing nearly 6 feet tall, the soft-spoken woman appeared in her mid-20s with skin as soft and smooth as rich, dark chocolate.

Trying not to stare, Brett asked, "What does it mean?"

"It means I see you. I recognize you as the worthy person before me."

"And how would you know that?"

She only smiled. "Do you mind?" she asked, gesturing to the blanket he sat on.

"Knock yourself out. I've got **nothing to lose**."

Arranging her long, flowing skirt around her ankles, she raised kohl-lined eyes to gaze into what felt like his very soul.

"You have yet to **discover** it."

"Okay, Mystery Lady, what have I 'yet to discover'?"

"If I tell you, it is my discovery, and not yours."

"Look, I don't know what your game is but I am not big in the patience department right now. So why don't you tell me what you want or take your pretty little ass off my blanket and move down the **concrete** path to the exit."

Adjusting her legs in a **yoga**-like position, Mystery Lady reached out a long-fingered hand, covering Brett's in a cupped shell of velvet warmth.

"Search your heart and you shall discover it."

Captured in her hypnotic stare, any words he had froze in a throat gone dry. Slowly rising with the grace of a dancer, she smiled that sweet, knowing smile.

"Sawubona, Brett. Look to your heart."

And then she was gone. How had she known his name?

"I've got to stop hitting those **after hours** bars."

Shaken more than he cared to admit, Brett rose and shook out the blanket. Packing it, and the little he brought with him, Brett worked his way to his home away from home. **Home alone** – again.

A **landslide** of emotions crowded his mind. Had he imagined the encounter on the beach? Maybe his lieutenant knew how on edge Brett was, how much he needed the time away.

Leaving Moonlight Bay, Brett walked past Old Highway 101 and the **library**, tucked across from Viewpoint Park.

Brett had grown up in Encinitas and it always felt like home. Maybe that was why he chose this place to heal.

Unlocking the door of his rented studio, Brett tossed the blanket across a chair. Puzzling over thoughts of his Mystery Lady, Brett decided it was time to shut it down. Like a kid in need of **nap time**, he stretched out on a bed designed for something smaller than his 6 foot 4 inch frame.

Closing his eyes, the whispered sound soothed him off to sleep – Sawubona, Brett.

Challenge #4

Gold Rush

Only **time will tell** if he made the right decision. It wasn't exactly what his lieutenant had in mind when he ordered homicide detective, Brett Connors, to take some time off. Standing before the lieutenant was his best detective, telling him he wanted to quit.

"Hell, Brett. If I'd known you'd come back from Encinitas with this in mind, I would have handcuffed you to your desk."

"You're not my type, LT. I prefer the ladies – **experience preferred**."

"Funny, Connors. Why don't you give it some time? Think it over."

"I have thought it over. I need out while I'm still known as a decent cop."

Try as he might, the lieutenant could not talk Brett out of it. Assured his job would always be there in San Francisco, Brett sold most everything he owned. If he could figure out a way to nail **plywood** over the pain, he would have done that, too.

His last case left major scars. It was always like that with the murder of a child. But, this one really got to him. Maybe he was having his own mid-life crisis. Now 46, he married young and divorced not long after – a common casualty of cops.

So here he was, flying down the coast – a coastal ride to turn the tide. "Maybe my new career will be a goddamn **poet**," he smirked. Brett floored the pedal of his vintage Mustang, the one he nicknamed ***Gold Rush***.

He didn't know what his new life **scenario** would be. He had a healthy nest egg, thanks to his grandmother, Nana Connors. She raised Brett when his mother died from an overdose. He had no idea who is father was, and could care less about his identity. He promised himself he would never throw away his kid – if he ever had one.

With that thought, the image he could not erase appeared once again. With cruel, Technicolor recall, the crimson canvass painted all the intricate detail of a lifeless, 7-year-old child. The image brought its usual **influx** of rage and pain.

Abruptly jerking the steering wheel, Brett pulled *Gold Rush* to a halt on a bluff overlooking the Pacific. **Winter** was coming. The once **velvet** touch of the ocean air slapped against the door, serving as a **road block,** preventing escape. Escape. Now there's a thought.

======

Challenge #5

Building Sandcastles

BRETT'S **SEARCH** FOR HIS new home had not taken long. It was as if the small bungalow had his name written all over it. Built in 1955, it was a short block from the beach, in the Leucadia community of Encinitas, California – in the north county of San Diego. Thanks, in part, to the small fortune his grandmother left him, Brett made the realtor's day by paying cash.

Sitting in a beach chair, not far from a **danger zone** for crashing waves, Brett monitored the kids building sandcastles. Wondering where the heck the parents were, his protective mode was on full throttle. With **sun rays** bouncing off his Ray-Bans and a five-day growth of beard, Brett had the dangerous look of a **gunslinger** bent on trouble. He wore the look naturally, like a second skin or a shield of **armor**.

The faint hint of a smile broke through as he watched the small boy run over to him and ask, “You want to play with my Buzz Lightyear?”

“That is a pretty cool **astronaut**.”

“He’s not an astronaut,” the boy bristled, “He’s a space ranger.”

“Ah, a space ranger. That’s much cooler than an astronaut.”

“Damn straight,” the boy responded.

That brought a burst of laughter from Brett. It had been a long time when he could laugh so easily.

“Michael James, get over here right this second!”

Rolling his eyes in a male conspiratorial expression, the boy whispered, “That’s my Mom.”

“Michael James...”

With an audible sigh, he turned his head and yelled, “Coming, Mom.”

Turning back with a mischievous grin, the boy raised his hand in the universal high-five and said, “See ya’.”

Slapping the small hand, Brett chuckled, “See ya’, buddy.”

He watched the boy join his Mom and the little girl he assumed was the boy's sister. Prancing up and down, next to Mom, was a white **poodle** – definitely a chick dog. He'd bet cold hard cash, it wasn't the boy's choice.

As if in **retaliation**, the poodle lifted its leg on Brett's blanket as the family parade made their way across the beach. Roaring in laughter, Brett warmed at the sound of the little boy's giggle.

With a quick jerk on the boy's arm, his mother pulled the boy along to a waiting **limousine**. "Welcome to southern California," Brett laughed.

Slowly the smile faded as he was transported back to the dark recesses of his mind. He saw the murdered child, who was only slightly older than the boy on the beach. Headlines of **journalism** trash screamed the ugly truth, if only in his head – THOU SHALT NOT KILL – OOPS – I DID.

Challenge #8

Win for the Good Guys

One thing leads to another and suddenly you have a new job. Not entirely sure if that was a good thing, Brett Connors returned to the only thing he really knew – being a cop. Once more, Brett held the shield for a homicide detective.

Shedding the **ruffian** look he'd worn for the last six months, his return was like an old pair of jeans – worn around the edges but more comfortable than anything else.

He spent 25 years as a detective in San Francisco, a city always controversial, like the **extrovert** sibling caught between **tranquility** and chaos.

Too much isolation with **unlimited access** to the ugly side of life was the perfect recipe for collapse. That had been Brett's life. It all came crashing around him with the death of an innocent child.

He left San Francisco. He left the force, and he nearly left his life. He moved back to the place of his childhood home, back to Encinitas, California. He regretted the changes, especially the loss of his grandmother, Nana Connors. He really could use the comfort of one who always loved him.

Nana had been his **lantern** in the dark feelings of an abandoned child. He never knew his father. His mother's drug-filled world barely slowed to give him birth and she paid the ultimate price of abuse.

"God, get over yourself," Brett grumbled.

His slide down the dark corridors of despair had kicked Brett into action. He made the call back to his life. The Encinitas homicide division was glad to have him and Brett hoped it was the right thing to do. So far, he skirted any suggestions of a meeting with the precinct's shrink.

Placing his beer mug in the top rack, Brett pressed the On button, releasing the soft, and strangely comforting sound of the **dishwasher**. Peering out the kitchen window, he watched the stealthy movement of a slinking cat. Crouching, waiting, the cat pounced. With a wild flap of wings, the bird barely escaped the **coffin** trap of the feline felon.

"Another win for the good guys," Brett reflected.

Maybe it was a sign. God had removed the **barrier**, as if to say, "**Read between the lines**." Life goes on.

Challenge #9

Offended by Murder

HOMICIDE DETECTIVE, BRETT CONNORS, had never been much of a **daydreamer**. Long before he collected his shield, Brett knew the harsh reality of life. He'd seen a mother trapped by the ugly **silkworms** of drugs, spinning their lying silken threads of promise.

People were always looking for **painkillers**. If **you got lucky**, you found someone special to help you through the pain. For Brett, that had been his grandmother. If not for her, he probably would have ended up on the other side of the shield.

Crouching over the body of one of the beach's homeless, Brett hoped she was finally home, in a better place. The **catcall** of a senseless soul, tugged at Brett's need for justice. The arrogance of murder offended him. When no one else would take up the cause, Brett made it his mission to bring dignity to life.

The sun slept beneath the ocean floor. Murder didn't wear a wristwatch.

"Do you have a **phobia** about sleeping?" yawned Mark Johnson, the precinct's top criminal technician.

"It's overrated. What do you have?"

"Besides the **iron-ore** rock with dried blood and hair?" Mark smirked.

"Yeah, I think you could say we are on the same **wavelength** on that," Brett countered. "Besides the obvious, what else do we have?"

"She was hit several times with a **closed fist** and was probably the **desire** of a perverted killer."

"Mark, I wouldn't quit your day job."

Challenge #10

Don't Ask

After 25 years on the force, homicide detective, Brett Connors, had seen more than his share of depravity. It never ceased to amaze him how cruel humans could be to other human beings. Maybe that was a good thing. Brett hoped he never got used to the likes of the latest **sick fucker** terrorizing the quiet beach town of Encinitas.

Called the **Birdcage** Bandit by the local media, the serial killer once again left his calling card – a gilded birdcage ornament, dangling from the victim's big toe. The killer's propensity for dumping the body on one of Encinitas's eleven beaches kept little of his M.O. from the public eye. It added to Brett's problems in solving the crimes.

What started as an isolated case a year ago, had hit every form of media with the **culmination** of threats that "heads would roll" if the killer was not found. As the lead investigator, Brett became the **scapegoat**. **Little by little**, his private world ended and soon his image was on news shows nationwide. Us Weekly dubbed him “Maverick” from a photo taken of him on **horseback**. The paparazzi had invaded Brett’s final means of escape. And it pissed him off.

But, murder pissed him off more. There had been seven murders within the last year – a birdcage ornament hanging from each victim’s big toe. The killer, however, had secret messages hidden on each victim. Recently, he addressed them Dear Detective Maverick. Each time Brett found one, the rage inside him built. The latest message was written on an **ammonia**-soaked cloth, crammed in the victim’s mouth and secured with **bubble wrap** circling her head. The cloth was now laid flat on the coroner’s table.

Dear Detective Maverick: What have we here? As I dragged my knife across this poor girl’s lovely breasts, I could feel her heart beat right through my knife and up my arm. It seems I may have been a tad overzealous in my attempt to revive this poor girl from her ***irregular*** *heartbeat. I didn’t have any smelling salts so I used the ammonia. Alas, her heart beats no more. It’s what a whore deserves! Until next time...happy trails.*

P.S. I left you a sweet treat for all your hard work.

"Brett," the coroner murmured. "I think I found your sweet treat." He held out his forceps that held a cherry red **gumdrop**.

"Where did you find that?" Brett questioned.

"Don't ask."

Challenge #11

Deathtrap Chances

It was sheer **stupidity** for the Birdcage Bandit to keep playing his game. With each murder, he became increasingly bold, taking **deathtrap** chances with his life. But, where was it written that murder followed rules?

Homicide detective, Brett Connors, had been working the case for a year. Each time he thought he had the killer, he found another woman, murdered **in the name of love**. Or was that a game, too? The killer had called them whores, and his one true love. So much of it felt like he was playing them.

The press had a field day, speculating on the meaning behind the birdcage ornament, hanging from each victim's toe. Now, homicide had something new – something they kept from the press. Lying beside the bloodstained bed of the latest victim was a **switchblade**.

The Gray Titan with the **gunpowder**-colored handle was sold as “double edge, double action.” The coroner’s office confirmed this blade had seen a lot more than “double action.”

“Getting sloppy, asshole,” Brett murmured. Or had they gotten that close? At times, Brett swore he could feel the disturbed breath of the killer. What would they have found if they arrived five minutes sooner? Why didn’t he just **clobber** the doorman who stood in his way?

“Don’t go there – not yet,” Brett thought, but, it was hard not to. The latest victim was a **kindergarten** teacher, for God’s sake. What had she ever done but try to start a kid’s life out right? He could still hear the wails of her mother’s **sorrow**.

Witnesses saw someone running from the victim’s home. As was so often the case, the descriptions varied so much, you’d think an army of men had fled. He was bald – he had long hair. He had a **goatee** – he was clean-shaven. What they had in the description department was a whole lot of nothing. Ouija boards and insane **asylum** patients made more sense.

Somehow, Brett had to figure it out. It had gone on far too long. Far too many women had died. He couldn’t let it continue. He couldn’t destroy another family’s life.

Challenge #13

Rancid Side of Life

Brett wondered how he got involved in this world. He was pretty sure those who called San Diego, America's Finest City, had not strolled through this neighborhood.

This wasn't the home of high-priced **coke** dealers. Their clientele was up the coast, closer to where Brett worked as a homicide detective. It had been a long time since he had been to this part of San Diego, where cops were about as welcomed as a ship-bound **glacier** off the coast of Alaska.

He had the Birdcage Bandit to thank for his tour of this sad, **cesspool** life the city had thrown away. The serial killer had terrorized the north beach community of Encinitas for over a year now. There had been 12 women murdered – their bodies dumped on the beaches of Encinitas, like left-over trash from the Over-the-Line tournament.

The media, with all their irreverence, coined the Birdcage nickname. Derived from the discovery of a birdcage ornament left with each victim, Brett seethed at its dehumanizing mockery.

The case had earned Brett the 15 minutes of fame he never wanted, much to the delight of the killer. The media christened him Maverick, from a paparazzi shot of Brett riding a horse. He didn't know what he hated more, the incessant hounding of the media or the taunting notes the killer left at the crime scenes. It was the latest note that led Brett to this part of town.

Dear Detective Maverick:

I find it so entertaining to see how famous you have become. You should thank me, you know. Before me, you were a nobody – a worthless hack of a detective with all the appeal of an aging, balding ***womanizer****. You are such a loser!*

I am growing weary of our game. There is simply no challenge anymore. So, I'm upping my stakes. Take yourself south from the ocean shores. Travel to the ***rancid*** *side of life, where the toxic is laid to rest. You know it, don't you, Detective Maverick – the place where you can see the concrete underbelly of broken dreams, where many leap from their pathetic lives. Go to the* *place, sliced by 5 and forgotten by most. There you will find the answer. But, hurry. I will not be so generous again.*

"Barrio Logan," was what popped into Brett's mind. He'd bet his meager **paycheck** on it.

Interstate 5 cuts off the industrial and low-income community that is a couple of miles from downtown San Diego. All the clues were there. Barrio Logan became a dumping site for toxic waste in the early 1990s, and the Coronado Bay Bridge split the community in two. More than a few suicide jumpers took their final dive off that bridge.

"But, why here? Is he playing us again?"

Brett vowed it would end today. He would expose the killer as the **imposter** he was. The killer's **tablet**-sized notes of arrogance were really **just an illusion**. He was not the cunning, invincible portrait of evil. His overconfidence would blind him to his certain fate. It would end now, or Brett would abandon his **shield** for good.

Challenge #14

Soundless Scream

SITTING ON HIS DECK with feet propped on the railing, Brett took another sip of his lite beer, wishing it was **Simpatico** instead. The **velvet warmth** of the summer night drifted with the **fragrant** scent of flowers he couldn't name. He was weary deep into his soul. Twenty-five years as a homicide detective took its toll. He felt no joy in solving the Birdcage Bandit case. Too many had died before a judge sentenced the serial killer to life. He got life – more than you could say for his victims.

Shutting his eyes, Brett struggled to banish the visions from his mind – the **cupid**-shaped lips of the last victim frozen in a soundless scream.

Maybe because he was a cop, he felt the **trespass** of the **shadow** he did not see. Opening his eyes, he looked into the **luminescent** mirror of his soul. Had he found his **doppelganger** or had he finally lost his mind? Had some moment in time caused the **butterfly effect** that brought him here? And what did it all mean?

Challenge #15

Eyes of a Stranger

THEY WERE THE **EYES of a stranger**, yet one he knew all his life. In the background was the rhythmic sound of Mumbo **Gumbo**. That was strange. He never knew the band to travel from their northern California gigs. What were they doing in San Diego's north county city of Encinitas?

Vanishing like a street vendor's **contraband** CD, the soulful sounds faded as if they were never there. Rising into view was a **meadow** of softly, swaying wheat. Kissed with the **shimmer** of sunlight, and bowing in silent reverence, it formed a radiant tunnel of invitation.

Brett blinked in disbelief – the eyes of the stranger. The sweet, half smile did little to cover the **nude** loveliness, as she stretched her hand to his. Afraid to breathe, Brett whispered, "Who are you?"

"Let it go, Brett. Let it **fall on me**," slowly she rose, and rose.

Bursting from the wheat of ocean blue, the **dolphin** danced on the crest of waves, to the sound of a wailing sax.

Sitting up in bed with the sheets twisted around his heated body, Brett shook off the absurdity of dreams. Maybe this was a message that he was just one more **sidestep** removed from **death**. If heaven looked like this, what was he waiting for?

Challenge #17

Funny Place

The tipped glass of **red wine** flowed over the purity of the white linen, forming single drops of escape. Swallowed by the pooling blood, the drops surrendered to the silent thirst.

Following the path, he dipped his finger across the mingled crimson and raised it to lips gone dry. A **hurricane** of emotion shook him, as it always did. From his early days when he learned **scary monsters** were more than a child's imagination, he fought hard for control. Never again would he be the victim. If he had to kill them all, so be it.

Pulling the aging **photograph** from his inside pocket, he pressed it against the slow beating of his heart and began to cry. Why was there always so much **drama**? If only they wouldn't make him so mad.

***

Brett received the call shortly before three a.m. At that hour, he knew someone else had died. That was his job. That was his life. There was no **prophylactic** cure for the atrocity of murder, and it never got easier. Making his way toward the **morgue**, Brett prayed it never did.

With Metallica blasting in **hysterical**, ear-splitting volume, Brett waved his hand in front of the face of the city's coroner, Randy Watkins.

"Yo, Randy, how the hell can you hear yourself think?"

Picking up a remote, Randy silenced his ironic song selection, *And Justice For All.*

"We're talking classic here," Randy smiled, "Anyway, my guests don't seem to mind."

"Well, if any of them raise a hand in protest, let me know. What's the word on my Jane Doe?"

Rolling his **wheelchair** over to an adjacent table, Randy pointed to her lower back.

"Here's something that might interest you."

Leaning close, Brett murmured, “What is that? A faded tattoo?

“More like a **stain**.”

“You mean a birthmark?”

“No, I mean a stain.”

“So, what is it?”

“Elementary, my dear Watson. It’s hair dye.”

“Funny place for hair dye.”

“Exactly.”

Challenge #18

Too Late

After his last serial murder case, Detective Brett Connors took a much-needed break. He climbed into his fully restored 1965 Ford Mustang Coupe with the vintage pony seats, reveling in the power of more than 3000 **Revolution**s Per Minute. A **vagrant** traveler caught in a **riptide** of emotions, Brett discovered **it's hard** to outrace your thoughts – even at **lightning** speed.

As he drove past hillsides **lush** from winter rains, his thoughts whispered, "**do you hear me?**" But, it wasn't his voice he heard. It was the voice of a killer. The sound of one so **evil**, one so vile, his acts ranked their own brand of **felony**. In his **gut**, Brett knew the hollow pain of arriving too late. He knew no matter how far he traveled or how fast he drove, he could never turn back the clock. He would always arrive too late.

Challenge #19

Turn Back Time

BRETT WATCHED THE FOG roll in to swallow Morro Rock. It was surreal to watch a nearly 600-foot volcanic plug disappear. It was time travel without the machine.

"**If I could turn back time**," Brett thought, "I'd get there before the first **slaughter**."

That's how he thought of his last murder case – senseless slaughter. His heart still ached with the **residue** of hopelessness he felt as he raced against **lunacy**. Brett would never forget that last day, the day the killer died.

Sobbing like a child as he mistook Brett for the **tyrant** of his past, he huddled in a corner with his arm wrapped around his latest victim. Brett arrived too late to save her. Like the others, she would never know the simple **luxury** of a caring touch, the warmth of a San Diego ocean breeze.

He was no **foreigner** to the macabre, but this killer took it to another level. Her vacant stare of death silently told the story of a madman. Drained of life, they took no relief in the vanishing of the horrific scene. Brett almost envied her loss.

Brett could still hear her scream as he pounded up the stairs. His heart racing like a **cocaine** hit, he had **broken** down the door. But he was too late. Her severed hand still held the glass of red wine as blood and wine mixed in a trail of no direction.

"Don't touch me. Do you hear me? Don't touch me," sobbed the hysterical cry of a killer, trapped in the past.

"She made me do it. They always make me do it. Why? Why"

With a shriek of madness, he charged. The bullet of the police **sniper** spun him around and there he fell – his hand touching one of another – accepting a last glass of wine.

Challenge #21

Nowhere to Go

LIKE MOST ADULTS, BRETT's taste in music was stuck back in his teenage era. His collection of CDs was **totally 80s**, totally rock.

It was a **miracle** he survived those years. He kept the collection as a pounding reminder. It amused him that the younger guys at the precinct might think him a **dinosaur**, but appreciated the Boss, U2, Queen and the other legends of the time.

Propping his feet on his deck railing, Brett smiled at the memory of his grandmother, Nana Connors, warning a 17-year-old Brett of the dangers of getting a **tattoo**.

"You might think they look cool now but just wait until you get to be my age. There's **shrinkage** and they're not exactly **reversible**. Not to mention you wouldn't live long afterwards, 'cause I'd kill you for getting one."

Brett chuckled, remembering it all started when he admired the knife and heart tattoo of **Poison** band member, Bret Michaels. God, he missed Nana. She was his rock, when no one else cared.

It was a rare day off from his job as a homicide detective in the north coastal community of Encinitas. His plan was to do absolutely nothing. From his deck, he watched some new construction going up, half a block from his beach bungalow.

He watched a worker lift the handles of a **wheelbarrow**, piled high with gallons of **epoxy** paint, his muscles straining with the load.

Brett loved the idea that he had nowhere to go, nothing to do. It was a **dreamland** he had not visited in much too long.

Challenge #22

Don't Turn Around

THE DARK, STARLESS NIGHT sucked the very breath out of him. The only sound was his labored breathing as he fought to regain control. How did he let this happen? He had the killer in his sight and then he simply vanished. With his Glock 23 poised and ready, Brett strained to pick up something – anything – through the blanket of darkness.

Then he heard it – a click right behind his left ear. "**Don't turn around**," the voice rasped. Complete **rage** enveloped him. How did he let this asshole sneak up on him? He wasn't a **candy**-assed rookie. He knew how to **play** the game.

"Drop your gun on the ground – nice and easy."

Brett's mind raced as he weighed his options. He didn't need a **recap** of what a cold-hearted bastard the **Mischief** Maker was. Every **tabloid** out there took perverse pleasure in front-page features of the killer that had circulation soaring.

"**Don't tell me** – my cocked gun in your ear affected your hearing. I said drop your gun. Unless the next sound you want to hear is a **harp**, don't get any **crackpot** notion that you have any other option. Do it –now!"

Challenge #23

The Senselessness

It's funny the places your mind goes when you have a cocked gun in your ear. Homicide detective, Brett Connors, sadly, was finding that out. Maybe he had lost his mind, or at least he was **half way there**.

Faced with the **primitive** need for survival, Brett had the crazy thought that he wished he worn a helmet from a **spacesuit**. Totally nuts.

Tracking him **all night long**, Brett had lost sight of the killer, dubbed the Mischief Maker. Now, here he was, a cocked gun in his ear, his own Glock 23 on the ground and Brett thinking about spacesuits.

The Mischief Maker's last victim had been a single mom, working as a **waitress** to keep food on the table for two young boys. A high school **dropout**, she had worked hard to give her sons a better life. The senselessness is what drove Brett. He'd be damned if the killer would walk free. Unfortunately, him being damned looked a lot more likely at the moment.

Absently rubbing the St. Michael badge **medallion** his Nana had given him, Brett silently admonished, "Focus."

"Keep your hands where I can see them."

"**Relax**. I'm unarmed. Take a **tranquilizer**. I'll wait"

"You are in no position for jokes, Detective."

"Who's joking?" With a sudden thrust, Brett smashed the butt of his hand into the killer's nose, driving it into his skull. With his other hand, he chopped across his throat. Flipping him to his stomach, Brett handcuffed his wrists.

Pressing his knee into his back, rasping for breath, the anguished cries of the killer fueled Brett's need for revenge. He shook with the struggle for control.

"I hope they fry your ass. Plan on plenty of **solitude** in hell – and remember who sent you there."

Challenge #25

Seize the Moment

WHAT WAS HE DOING here? He was a homicide detective, not a frickin' hostage negotiator.

"Come on, tell me what you want. You want a car? **You want it? You got it!** Is that what you want? You have the **ransom** money. Seems all you need is a car to drive away."

"Shut up. I'm the one giving orders, Detective Connors. You better remember that."

The **mania** of the moment threatened to overpower Brett. The kidnapper was inside with a 20-pound-plus bag of bills, and a knife held to the victim's throat. Einstein hadn't counted on the cops disabling his car. That's when he started making demands.

His first was to bring Detective Brett Connors to the scene. Brett had no idea why.

"Okay, you're in charge. What do you want?"

"I want you, Detective. I'll let the girl go in exchange for you."

Well that was an interesting request. At 46, Brett thought he was getting too old for this shit. But, he knew he'd do whatever he had to so the girl could go unharmed.

"You got it," Brett replied.

"Don't be a hero, Connors," the task force leader growled.

"Look, if we don't seize the moment, **it's gone** – in a **nanosecond**. What, I should be a **coward**? What would Dirty Harry say?" Brett smirked.

"You ain't no Dirty Harry. **Throttle** back until we figure something out."

Brett was already surveying the surroundings. It was a quiet neighborhood –where kids had **lemonade** stands and shot hoops. Now, it had an invasion of cop cars, helicopters and media vans.

Taking a **vault** over the hood of his car, Brett walked towards the house.

"Connors, get your ass down!"

“Hey, I’m coming in. Then you let her go”

He was on **robot** control, moving and reacting to the showdown he created.

Challenge #27

Shattered Hope

BRETT WATCHED WITH **FASCINATION** as the kidnapper approached him. His **stance**, deceivingly relaxed, Brett's survival instincts tested the limits of **patience**.

"I'm here, like you asked. Now, let her go."

The slender, young man tightened his chokehold on the trembling, pale girl, pressing the knife along her throat.

"I told you, I give the orders!"

Brett held up his hands in **cult**-like reverence.

"Easy, man. What do you **propose**?"

"I 'propose' that you die today," he sneered. With that, he swept the knife across the girl's throat, releasing a sound of misery, more wrenching than the cry of a lone **wolf**.

Shots rang out, dropping the young man to blanket the innocent victim. Brett stood frozen with the horror he had caused. Later he would wonder what he should have done. For now, all he could be was a cop.

"**Be yourself**. Do your job," he thought, fighting to block any feeling. **Police** were running around him, but he did not see them. The shrieking disapproval of a **seagull** flying overhead went unheard. All faded, but for the youthful crumple of shattered hope.

As he bent down, the CD of his mind softly played,

If you see me getting by, If you see me getting high, ***Knock me down.***[1]

---

1. Red Hot Chili Peppers, "Knock Me Down," track 2 on *Mother's Milk*, EMI Records, 1989, compact disc [or streaming audio, Spotify/Apple Music].

Challenge #29

Departure

It was after **midnight**, a time for **divine voices**, offering **charm** and the relief of all **sensation**. **Yes**, it was **departure**, but it was a welcome alternative to the **domino** tumble of troubled memories.

Brett dreamed of a simple life, somewhere in the **Canary** Islands or other far-off places. Instead, his mind locked like the shutter of a **camera**, captured the stark reality of death.

Challenge #30

Damning Tears

WITH **RAIN** TRACKING DOWN the window like damning tears from his soul, he wondered, "**What have I done?**" His thoughts could not silence the constant pinging of his **triangle** of doubt. "Would you **change your mind**, if you had a second chance?"

His life as a homicide detective brought many gut-wrenching decisions into his life – none more difficult than this one. With the **out-of-order** kaleidoscope of events tumbling before the back screen of his mind, the scenes went straight to the **heart** like a heat- seeking **missile**. The pain was an almost **fantastic** relief to the **atomic** pressure he felt from a **picture** playing over and over and over.

Challenge #31

Unrelenting Lyrics

He could **scout** for answers, but the questions would **never stop**. All Brett could do was take one day at a time – **so far so good**. Or was it? Most days, Brett questioned if he could go on. The thread was **hair**-thin.

The **digital** clock screamed 3 A.M. Surrendering all thought of sleep, Brett made his way to the kitchen. The room held the **stink** of neglected trash and unwashed dishes.

Bracing his hands against the sink, he waited for the **unavoidable** pain of nocturnal memories. Like unrelenting **lyrics** stuck in his head, the vision pounded against his mind. His **pulse** joined in a corresponding beat. It was an **infection** he could not cure.

Challenge #33

A Place to Hide

HOMICIDE DETECTIVE, BRETT CONNORS, would rather be naked and strung across a sea of scorpions. Instead, he was sitting, cooling his heels in the office of the precinct's shrink.

"**If you leave** now, you can come up with an excuse later," he plotted.

Only his **future** as a cop was in jeopardy. He'd trade that right now for **a place to hide**. **Fate** had put him on this **ride**. He didn't need a shrink to confirm that.

Besides he had an **avalanche** of paperwork he hadn't touched. He could **do without** the relentless reminders of things best forgotten – the kind of things illuminated **in the dark** of night. It was time for a **break away**, one far away from his current **view** on life.

"Detective Connors, the doctor will see you now."

Challenge #35

Human Need

BRETT COULDN'T REMEMBER THE last time he felt the tug of sexual attraction. His world had not allowed anything as simple as human need. So, what were the odds – **one in a million?** Long-forgotten lust zeroed in on the precinct's shrink. Who said God didn't have a sense of humor?

It was tough enough trying to **pretend** that he spent the **night** sleeping, without slapping down Mr. Willy. Dr. Sweeney was a **load** of sensuality. Her auburn hair was sleeked back in a style that had Brett's finger itching to release it. Her eyes were a shade of green best left to a **fable** artist. **With or without** the enhancement of make-up, the long lashes, he knew, were her own.

"Which **victim** haunts you, Detective?"

The **squeeze** on his heart worked better than a cold shower. Yet, even over the drumming in his ears, he heard the whispered slide of **nylon** as the lovely doctor crossed her excellent legs.

"How could I select only one from such a **crowd**?"

Challenge #37

Troubled Soul

MAGGIE SWEENEY WAS BORN a mother. She nurtured the needy and loved the unloved.

She remembered telling her mother, "**When I grow up**, I'm going to have 7 children, one for each day of the week."

Her mother had laughed and said, "Thank goodness you aren't an annual thinker."

Maggie hadn't understood at the time, but she knew being a mother was her calling. **Just one thing**, God had not been on the same call. She felt the loss like a death in the family. At 42 and single, she let go of that dream long ago and created another.

She wasn't brave enough to work with children, but focused her life on caring and healing. She loved her work in psychology. She felt she made a difference, but she needed challenge. Her recent appointment as the Encinitas North County police psychiatrist, gave her that challenge in spades.

Cops were an interesting, complex test of wills. Some would **flirt**, some would rant and rave, while others sat in stony silence. So many walls, built to survive. Few would **sign** on for her help. It was a **slippery** slope, trying to help.

She thought of Brett Connors, a 25-year homicide detective who had seen more than any man should. He was 6 feet 4 inches of burning sexuality, without the arrogance. His black hair, sprinkled with just a kiss of gray, defied his 46 years of life. But his startling blue eyes told the story. Often, his gaze wandered **so far away**, Maggie wondered if she could call him back.

The end of their first session left her frustrated.

"And a good portion of it sexual," she confessed to her empty room. There was no use denying the hot **spice** of tingling waves the sexy detective stirred to life.

Okay, it was **wrong** – really wrong. Maggie would just have to douse those thoughts if she wanted to reach him. His troubled soul worried her. Her **fear** was she might be too late.

Challenge #39

Biggest Challenge

Terror had been a part of his dreams for so long that skipping sleep was **no problem**. In dreams, killers never died and victims died over and over.

While he thought he was **a little closer** to hiding his life, Brett's body betrayed him with the lines of sleepless nights. His **casual** style and dry humor was a mask he slipped on easily.

It helped him **float** by department shrinks, whenever protocol demanded a visit. He knew just how to **respond** to get a quick **release** back to the streets. But, that was before the precinct hired the lady shrink. Package that brain of hers with a whole lot of curves, and legs that went on **forever**, and Brett knew it spelled a whole lot of trouble.

In his **line** of work, Brett understood trouble, but he had no **doubt**, Dr. Margaret Mary Sweeney was going to be his biggest challenge yet.

Challenge #41

Killer Legs

"So WHEN ARE YOU giving me the green light, Doc?

Detective Brett Connors directed those ridiculously blue eyes at Maggie, the newly appointed psychiatrist for the North County police district.

"If I didn't know better, Detective, I'd think you didn't like talking to me."

"Hey, I'll talk all you'd like over drinks tonight – after I'm cleared to get back on the streets."

"Is that what it takes – a couple of drinks? Or is it something else? **Do you know?**"

Brett slammed the chair down he had been leaning back on.

"Don't **push** me, Doc, you wouldn't like the result."

"Is that what you think I'm doing? Pushing?"

"And stop that bullshit shrink-speak. Next, you'll be asking me, 'how does that make you feel?'"

Brett silently fumed at his loss of control. Brett's **quest** for control was a life-long challenge. If not for his grandmother, he had no doubt he'd be in prison or dead.

Like most cops, Brett hated the department shrinks always looking for **something more**, with their **phony** platitudes and **perfect** diction. But, then most of the previous shrinks were pasty placards, easily dismissed.

The same couldn't be said about Dr. Margaret Mary Sweeney. If he knew the lady shrink would visit his dreams, Brett might actually take up sleeping again. He'd do well to **remember** the **devil** wore many disguises – even if it had killer legs. It was really too bad this whole **scene** was such a **waste** of what he knew could be something explosive.

Challenge #43

Making Life Miserable

Maggie Sweeney wanted a challenge when she signed on as San Diego's North County Police psychiatrist, and she found one. The toughest part of her job was conducting a Psychological Fitness-for-Duty examination. Maggie understood what being a cop meant to the men and women she worked with.

She also understood the challenges. A cop wasn't seen as the fireman **hero** who raced into a building filled with **smoke** and fire. More often than not, the public viewed a cop as an **idiot** bent on making their life miserable.

Looking at her notes, Maggie had to **ponder** her **fortune** – or misfortune – depending on her point of view at the time, regarding the request for an FFD exam on Detective Brett Connors. A 25-year veteran, the detective, over the last few years, had been assigned to a series of horrific murders. It didn't take much **reflection** on Maggie's part to recognize a man in some serious pain.

Partly due to her profession, but more because of who she was as a person, the vortex of such agony sucked Maggie in. This is why she became a psychiatrist.

Now, if she could just get over this uncontrollable urge to **jump** the detective's bones.

"Let's just complicate the whole damn thing," Maggie mused.

She remembered when she **used to be** a rational person. She needed to find a way to **settle down** before her next **round** with the sexy, troubled Detective Connors.

Challenge #46

Slow Burn

DETECTIVE BRETT CONNORS REACHED for his **shirt** while trying to **gather** his control. Slipping the Chargers t-shirt over his head, he was fighting a losing battle to the **race** of angry thoughts.

He had fought hard to overcome the **compulsive** urge to smash his fist into his lieutenant's face when he was told he was on administrative leave for the next week. He did a slow **burn** while the lieutenant shifted uncomfortably in his chair.

"Look, Brett, be smart about this. Play the game and you'll be back on the streets in a week. After all, we can't have our **star**, Detective Maverick, on the sidelines. What would the press have to write about?"

Brett shifted a frigid, blue stare at his superior, his jaw clenched so tight, he felt the twitch of muscle snap against his temple.

"Okay, not funny, but you know this whole shrink-babble is **nonsense**. So, throttle back on that **temper** of yours and **think about it**. You visit the Doc a couple of times, dazzle her with that **sharp** mind of yours and kick back at the beach with a couple of Coronas for a few days."

Visit the Doc. Oh yeah, he'd visit one Dr. Margaret Mary Sweeney, Brett vowed silently. But it would be on his terms. It was all about control, baby.

Challenge #48

Forgotten Dreams

BRETT WATCHED THE SUN **seize** the darkness with its strong fingers of light. Taking a **swig** of beer, he toasted the breaking **dawn**.

The **popular** beach where he had his home was **clear** of any human form – just how he liked it. His **sour** thoughts quieted, waiting for the birth of a new day, comforted by the promise of hope. Here he faced the truth and found the embracing **gain** of forgotten dreams.

For his **part**, Brett could never play the political **fake** just to save his job. He was a cop, and no mask of any form could **overcome** the pain of a troubled life.

Challenge #50

Bent on Mischief

MAGGIE WALKED INTO D Street Café, searching the sports bar for her friends. The **press** of bodies in the place made for tough navigation. Feeling **lucky**, Maggie made a **turn** around the bar and finally spotted her three friends. At the same time, five-foot-nothing, Penny, placed her fingers between her lips and let out with a shrill whistle.

"Hey, Maggie, over here."

Blushing from her auburn roots to her toes, Maggie ignored the **provocative** stare of a guy in a Celtics jersey. She was a Lakers fan and this was finals night. He didn't have a prayer – on a sports level or a personal one.

Giddy with excitement, Penny raced over to her friend and gave her a hug belying her diminutive size.

"What took you so long to get here?" Penny shouted.

“A consultation with my boss took longer than I thought,” Maggie replied.

“Well, that’s un-American. Doesn’t he know it’s Game 7 of the NBA Finals? What’s the matter with him? He needs to get a life,” Penny whined.

Squeezing into the booth, Maggie shared hugs with Jane, a tall, slender blonde with the toned body of the marathoner she was.

Reaching over Jane, Sue Morris, Maggie’s life-long friend, hugged Maggie, uttering a sardonic, “Glad you could join us, Doctor.”

“Oh stop it, Sue,” Maggie smiled, “You can’t hold it **against** me that I take my job seriously.”

“Yeah, too seriously, if you ask me,” Sue replied.

“Well I didn’t. Hey, I got here before tip-off.” Gazing around the packed bar, Maggie observed, “This place is nuts.”

“Is that anyway for a psychiatrist to talk,” Penny giggled.

“Har-har. I’m officially off duty.”

“Well, good thing,” Jane replied. “You have a lot of catching up to do. We’ve been here since 4:00.”

"I kind of guessed that by Penny's red nose meter," Maggie chuckled.

"Hey, hey, it was sunny today," Penny countered, "and I took the ankle biters outside to run down their batteries."

Penny was a daycare teacher. Her small-framed exterior fooled more than one toddler bent on mischief.

Like Maggie, Penny never had children. She and her husband, Mark, had tried it all. At age 40, Penny stopped trying and resolved to live out her mother fantasy with other people's children. Maggie tried to talk to her about adopting, but Penny always changed the subject.

Maggie looked around the **cozy** table of friends and smiled. They were her anchor, her sanity in a bottle she kept wrapped in her arms. She cherished each and every one of them. Without them, her life was **flatter** than the failed joke it sometimes felt like. They helped heal her **tender** and battered heart.

"Whoa, if we could bottle that and sell it, we could all retire," Penny stared.

Wondering if Penny was reading her thoughts, Maggie asked, "What are you talking about, Penny?"

“It’s not ‘what’ but ‘who’ I’d like to know,” Penny replied, cocking her eyes over the **top** of Maggie’s shoulders.

Maggie turned and felt the lightening slice of the familiar sexy, blue stare of Detective Brett Connors.

Challenge #52

Cloak of Sanity

MAGGIE KNEW **ALL TOO well** that a lot was riding on how she would **react**. As much as she would love to **fill** her arms with the sexy, Detective Connors, she had to **divert** those feelings behind the professional cloak of sanity.

Maggie felt the **jolt** of her heart as the loud **cheer** erupted over the Lakers' comeback in a game that looked lost. She heard the collective **curse** of the Celtics' fans who watched destiny slip through their fingers with the added **ache** of the **club** losing to their hated rivals.

Maggie smiled as her friends grabbed her in a group **embrace**. Over her best friend's shoulder, she tracked the slow, troubled departure of a detective who had seen too much.

Challenge #54

Buried Pain

BRETT'S **RANDOM** SIGHTING OF the sexy Dr. Sweeney at the local sports bar had to **shatter** any thought he had of disinterest. **Apart** from her killer legs, her very un-doctor-like jeans cupped a really excellent ass.

Brett channeled much of his anger from his ordered leave, squarely on the shoulders of one Dr. Maggie Sweeney. He spent 25 years as a homicide detective and did not appreciate the resident shrink pulling the plug – even temporarily. Okay, sure, he had taken a six-month leave before, but that was on his terms.

Brett simply had no **answer** to what it was about the lady shrink that stirred up so much emotion.

"Yeah, no **rhyme** or reason, other than a **figure** that makes you want to drop her on the nearest flat surface."

So, maybe that wasn't entirely accurate. "Well, yeah," Brett thought, "I wouldn't **pass** up a chance for a little floor-sweeping sex," but that wasn't what really bothered him about the Doc.

It started with those guided, green missiles of hers she called eyes. They bore through the walls surrounding his soul and dragged the buried pain to the surface light of day. No matter how he'd try to **blank** out the past, the lady Doc found a way around it.

Brett knew he could not **ignore** the challenge any longer. He would have to face it head-on or **explain** to himself why he chose to run.

Challenge #56

Mystic Maggie

MAGGIE DREAMED OF ONE **big shot** – one she would **smash** past her friend, Sue, as she made a futile attempt at a return. This **whole** match, Maggie felt off – almost as if someone was staring at her. Every time she would make a **move**, the back of her neck tingled in a tension she could not describe.

Maggie felt the singing of the racquet's strings as she put all her **force** behind her serve. It was her best serve yet – if she was aiming for the net.

"You know, I think we should just **write** this game off," Sue hollered across the net. "Are you **sure** you want to be here?"

"I know – you couldn't **prove** it by my game. Sorry, Sue, I guess my mind is just not in it," Maggie apologized.

Sue walked up to the net. She lifted her sunglasses and Maggie's and looked into Maggie's troubled green gaze.

“What’s going on?”

“I don’t know what it is,” Maggie replied. “I just have the **sense** that something very **unusual** is going to happen.”

“Unusual, exciting or unusual, weird?”

“I don’t know, maybe unusual scary.”

Sue felt a tremble up the back of her spine. She didn’t like this. She’d known Maggie most her life.

If Maggie was having strange vibes, something was going on. After all, they hadn’t nicknamed her Mystic Maggie as a child because of exotic, gypsy looks. Freckle-faced, red-haired Maggie had an eerie way of sensing bad things before they happened.

“Let’s give this up and go grab a glass of wine,” Sue said.

“Now, that’s the best idea I’ve heard all day,” Maggie smiled.

The two friends gathered their gear and headed for the clubhouse while eyes devoid of light, followed in silent rage.

Challenge #58

Blackened Soul

In a place where the **guilty** look for solace, a silent figure moved through the shadows of the darkened church. As he tried to **distract** his mind from his racing heart, its relenting pounding hammered all sound of hope.

The church was empty, but for the accusing stares of religious symbols of all he was not. The pressure he felt was **astronomical** and he would **tremble** from the power they held.

Wrestling with the need to run, he knelt in defiance of his weakening state. It was always there – the **elephant** in the room – where he hid the **portal** to his blackened soul. The whispers shouted past his wall of evil, ripping an anguished cry through his tightened lips.

His **league** with the devil had no power in this holy place. His choked cries struggled past a **larynx** closed by a fist of remembered fright. Where was the **magic**? Where was the comfort of a forgiving heart?

Challenge #59

Master of His Trade

Tomorrow was the day. With the **smooth**, **automated** movements of someone who had done the task a million times, the killer laid out the tools of his trade.

Long, callused fingers stroked the SOG Seal Bowie blade, as if stroking the beast itself. His labored breathing broke the silence; his hands tingling in anticipation of the power that would soon be his.

Soon he would be a **legend**, a **master** of his trade, one **better** than all the rest. His **narrow**, **hard** gaze lifted to his walls, plastered with photos of his selected prey. He studied her. He knew her. She was his destiny.

Looking into the cracked dresser mirror, he admired the **size** of his body he had worked so hard to perfect. His strength and clever mind would inspire a **combination** of fear and respect. Respect. He smiled at the thought.

Challenge #61

Tomorrow

TOMORROW WAS THE DAY. Tomorrow, Detective Brett Connors returned to active duty.

He got the word from his lieutenant, and wondered why he had not heard from the precinct's shrink, Dr. Maggie Sweeney. He pictured her in one of her **fancy** suits, with those long legs meant for wrapping around a man's waist.

"Son of a bitch," he cursed as he nicked his chin with the **razor**. He'd best get off that line of thought until he was done shaving.

He felt an **attack** of anxiety he couldn't quite place. He had been a homicide detective for 25 years. He had never known any other life. And though he had seen more than any man should, he knew he would never **neglect** his commitment to the job. So why was he feeling so unsettled. Maybe it was because he acted like such a **fool** with the lady shrink.

Brett took a **nimble** leap away from those thoughts. God, he was like a man obsessed. Why couldn't he keep her out of his head – in more ways than one?

Maybe he was just **wired** about getting back to his **shift** – a routine to offer an escape. A job that definitely wasn't for the **squeamish**, and in that department, Brett felt no **threat**, and yet, there was something.

Challenge #63

A Captive in Darkness

She opened her eyes in darkness. Was she sick? She felt so strange, so disconnected.

Feeling a rush of nausea, she retched at the sour taste of something slicing at her mouth. It did nothing to silence her fear as she suddenly struggled against her bound wrists and feet.

Where was she? Did someone **abduct** her? Why couldn't she remember?

The gag mocked her muffled cries for help. Maybe this was a dream or a bad trip from the street drugs she used. It wouldn't be the first time her **addictive** behavior had gotten her in trouble.

Here she was, a **captive** in the darkness, without any idea how she got here. She tried to slow her racing breath as she gasped for air. It was so dark. She strained to identify any kind of **detail**, praying the darkness was just a **mimic** of blindness, and not the real thing.

"Think, think, think," she repeated.

What possible **motive** could anyone have for kidnapping her? God knew she didn't have any money or anything else of any value. She hoped that was their reason. It was better than considering something far more frightening.

She ran her fingers across some **pattern** she couldn't define. What was that? Again and again her fingers would **return** to trace over the pattern.

Suddenly, she gasped with recognition – they were letters.

Her less than **steady** fingers traced the **sturdy** carvings. She jumped, as if burned, when her mind read the silent message – D-I-E-W-H-O-R-E.

Challenge #65

Dance Without Sound

LET THE GAMES BEGIN. It was time to leave his first **clue**. The killer lifted his victim's lifeless body, wrapping her in a final macabre **dance** without sound.

Driving in a race against dawn, the killer glanced at the illuminated **dial** of the clock. "There's time. So much time," he muttered.

Hints of dawn created a **divide** between the secrets of darkness and the horror of a new day. A thick **fog** clung to the darkness in its final grasp of evil. The sad, **lonely** sound of a crying seagull pierced the early hour.

It took him to another day. Another horror. One he tried never to **recall**. But, it was always there – a constant **reminder** of what he never had. The **rough** edges of memory sharpened into focus and silently he wept. This is what brought him here. This was his **torch** to bear. Let the games begin.

Challenge #67

Plastic Tomb

BRETT COULD ONLY IMAGINE the **agony** this poor girl had gone through. The **double** binding had sliced through her wrists from a last, desperate struggle for freedom.

Her eyes, **frozen** in a sightless stare, brought an **instant** chill, no matter how many times Brett saw that same lifeless look. The eyes of the dead haunted him in his 25-years as a homicide detective. They all asked the same soundless question – why?

The waves from Mission Bay stretched long ocean fingers closer to where the body was half-buried.

"Hey Johnson, you'd best get your butt in **motion** before the Pacific swallows your evidence," Brett chided.

"Genius doesn't let a little thing like an ocean get in the way," the technician smirked.

"Well, Genius, unless your middle name is Moses, kick it up a notch."

Slipping under the **oval** confinement of the roped-off area, Brett walked over to the young man, shivering on the boardwalk's wall. It was more than the early morning chill that had his body shaking in an uncontrollable dance.

A blanket of fog hid the **royal** blue of the ocean, covering it in shades of mourning. Brett waited as the early morning runner shifted his troubled gaze to his.

"Who could do such a thing?" His voice choked by a sense of horror.

"As a **rule**, I'd say far too many. I'm **sorry**, but I need to ask you some questions."

The runner shifted his gaze to **track** the slow progress of the body, now wrapped in its plastic tomb.

"Catch the bastard," he whispered.

"That's the plan."

Challenge #69

Let the Games Begin

He told himself he was not **anxious** for a response. He was in control. It was his game, his rules. He did not need their validation. No, he would control the game. When he thought of the **chain** of events leading up to this moment, the emotion was almost too much to bear.

Looking over at the tall, slender woman, bound and gagged, he ran a long finger down the smooth surface of the Bowie blade. Smiling with **coercive** diplomacy, his heart quickened at the visible shaking of her body. And, such a fine body it was. Hers was not a **conventional** beauty, but indeed, she was beautiful.

Setting the knife aside, he slowly moved to her side. Reaching down, he grasped the dangling electrodes and attached them one by one. Muffled cries mixed with tears of torture, but this was his game. The anticipation of the agonizing **current** was almost as entertaining as the act itself. It brought such a sweet **disposition** to the game.

He loved the **dynamic** of each new player. Each brought her own style, her own **inward** fears, her own **social** grace.

He lifted the pure white lily from its glass embrace. Holding it by its thick, long **stalk**, he laid it across the trembling woman's lap, and ran that same hand gently down her smooth, pale cheek.

"Let the games begin," he whispered.

Challenge #71

Blissful Sleep

WASN'T IT SWEET IRONY how **alive** he felt? A soft wind stirred the **dust** surrounding the lifeless body into a dreary cloud of **gloom**. Many thought him **mad**. He thought he was God.

He felt the power surge through his body and closed his eyes to witness his own **mirage** of pleasure. He smiled to think how well he planned. While the cops bumbled along, trying to solve the puzzle **piece** he left with the first victim, he had moved on.

Soon he could **sleep** a blissful sleep. But first, he must **tackle** the task at hand. Opening his eyes, he slowly moved to the frozen relic of beauty left behind. His **tendency** was to move swiftly, but he took a moment.

"**Welcome** to the moment of truth, " he whispered. "Too bad you won't be witnessing my glory."

Challenge #73

Ominous Sound

Maggie gasped awake in sudden awareness. What was that? She struggled for clarity through the depth of darkness surrounding her.

It sounded like a **thud**, like something dropped. But what? More than a little afraid to **pop** out of bed to investigate, Maggie waited for her eyes to adjust to the darkness.

The rhythmic ticking of her wall clock produced an ominous sound as its **pendulum** swung slowly back and forth.

Carefully placing one foot on the chilled **linoleum** floor, Maggie reached for her robe. She wasn't **fond** of the idea of looking out, but knew she had to if she wanted any more sleep that night.

Maggie chided herself for being such a **hysteric**. She lived in a gated community and the balcony was on the second floor of her tri-level. It was probably just a dream – a very real-feeling dream.

And then she heard it. Okay, maybe a **smidgen** of hysteria was in order. It had the eerie sound of a madman's **giggle**, followed by a strange **intonation** she could not define.

Scrambling away from the sliding glass door, Maggie's body shook from the helpless feeling of one so alone. She jumped in fear at the sound of a car engine igniting and the slap of headlights across the darkened room.

She sat frozen in the middle of her bed, her breath rasping in search of air. Was he gone? Was the madman gone? Much later, she would wonder in **retrospect** how she had known he was mad.

Challenge #75

Vault of Horror

MAGGIE LISTENED TO THE fading sound of the car driving away from the complex. She wouldn't be having any **sleepy** dreams tonight. With her heart pounding, she slowly approached the sliding glass door on her bedroom's balcony.

She didn't know why she was so frightened. There was no way to **ascend** to the second floor without a long ladder. That's what her brain told her, but the fear left an **acidic**, coppery taste in her mouth. Her pulse raced like her worst case of **sugar** high.

Reaching out trembling fingers, Maggie pushed one long slat of the blinds aside, desperately trying to **retain** some form of dignity as she grasped the front of her nightshirt. It was so dark. The light from the parking lot did little to illuminate the night. Bolstering her courage, Maggie felt her breath **contract** into a strangled hold.

She reached for the door, releasing the **outdated** latch. She'd have to replace that – soon. The door groaned in an agonizing **comment** on the early morning hour. Maggie's best **estimate** was it was around 3 AM.

"Get a hold of yourself," Maggie chided herself.

Why was she so frightened? She was a strong woman. Her friends called her the **original** Lone Ranger.

Sliding the heavy door along its track, Maggie shivered with the chill from the fall ocean air.

She stumbled back, gasping as her eyes landed on the sightless mass that was once a woman.

"Oh my God, oh my God."

The blinds crashed through the opening, as if their long-fingered reach would pull the body in from the cold. With tears streaming, Maggie felt hysteria snatching at the vision captured in an eternal vault of horror, now pressed into the recesses of her soul.

"911. What is your emergency?"

Challenge #77

Wet Remembrance

She was afraid to close her eyes. Maggie feared the grisly sight would do a slow **crawl** from its banished depth, once more taking center stage. But, she was so weary – mind, body and soul-weary.

The adrenaline rush of the last several hours had gone, leaving her feeling very vulnerable – definitely not what she needed when confronting Detective Brett Connors.

The chaos of the early morning had slowed to the silent beat of the red flashing lights of some of Encinitas' finest. It was all so surreal.

Maggie's body automatically tensed as she heard the familiar deep cadence of the detective's voice that signaled his return. She raised troubled green eyes, desperately fighting fatigue and finding his blue answering response.

"Doc, let's go over it one more time."

"Just what good do you think that will do," Maggie sighed, "the poor woman will not be any less dead, Detective."

"You know how it works, Doc. If you want us out of your hair, let's go through it again."

"**If that's what it takes**. What do you want to know?"

"Start with what woke you up."

Brett watched Maggie struggle to pull on her professional cloak of armor. He didn't know why he found it so damn stimulating.

"I heard a loud noise – a thump. I wasn't sure if it was a dream or if I actually heard something outside."

"What did you do next?"

"I decided to **wait** to see if I heard it again. Then I saw the car lights flash across the bedroom."

"What time was that?"

"I don't know –my guess is maybe 2:30, 3:00. I couldn't **bring** myself to turn on the light."

Brett watched her brow **wrinkle** in concentration and had an almost irresistible urge to smooth it away with a soft kiss. Oh for God's sake, this obsession had to stop.

"I walked over to the blinds and looked out. It was so dark. When my eyes adjusted, I saw, " her voice hitched with a soft gasp. Brett watched her rib cage rise with her deep breath as she started again.

"I saw what I thought was a bag of trash. I thought it was kids, pulling some kind of prank by throwing **junk** on my balcony."

Her eyes narrowed with wet remembrance of the **total** lack of dignity for the vessel that once held a precious life. Trying to **emerge** from misery's strong hold, Maggie finished the story with the flat tone of a clinical report.

Her **steep** shift in tone had Brett admiring her ability to pull herself together – under the most trying of circumstances. After all, it's not every day you get a corpse of a woman with no eyes dumped on your balcony.

"**Anything** else, Detective?"

Challenge #79

Castle of Peace

THE KILLER BEGAN TO **wash** the **sticky** traces of blood from his hands. Staring at the imagined stain, he washed again and again, uttering a **soft** admonition, "Wash your hands, William. You are such a dirty, little boy."

When his hands began to bleed, he reached for a **tube** of ointment. **Instead** of remorse, he felt calm, as he slowly traced the river's path of blood. He closed his eyes to escape to his **castle** of peace, where his **bundle** of conflict unraveled in the order of the truly mad.

He would not be ignored. **Stone** by stone, he would build his monument of glory. Body by body, he would get closer to his final reward. He would **challenge** fate and win.

"**Notice** me now, Dr. Sweeney?"

Challenge #81

Respect and Dignity

DETECTIVE BRETT CONNORS PUSHED on the door to the morgue. No matter how many times he had been there before, he was never ready for the slap of the strong, antiseptic smell – or the ear-splitting sound of Metallica blasting across the room.

Snatching the remote, Brett slammed the room into silence.

"Every time I come in here, I promise myself that I will not make a reference about the music being loud enough to wake up the dead."

"Yet, every time, you do, Brett. You need a new line."

"No, Randy, you need to get beyond your teenage years."

Randy Watkins was the city's coroner. Confined to a wheelchair from those teenage years did nothing to slow him down. Brett often wondered if his chosen career stemmed from the auto accident that crippled Randy and took the life of his friend. But, that one was best left to the lady shrink.

"That's not my vic."

"No, indeed. This **corpulent** fellow is far from the slender lady you brought me."

Furrow after furrow of fat spread itself across the coroner's table like the escaping layers of a baker's unrolled dough. The layers deformed his back like an old lady's **dowager**'s hump.

"Let me just **don** this gentleman in his **opulent** and **resplendent** cloak, and we'll take a look at your lady," Randy said while gently pulling the white sheet to the deceased's chin.

That was something Brett always appreciated about Randy – the respect and dignity he gave to those who no longer felt.

Rolling over to another draped figure, Randy slowly pulled the sheet back on the latest victim. Brett could only feel relief that the poor woman no longer suffered.

Her body showed signs of severe abuse and her eyes had been carved away with a surgeon's precision.

"What can you tell me, Randy?"

"Mark will have to confirm, but it appears she had several drugs in her body. The burn marks look like electrical shock, and the eyes were not taken by an amateur."

Lifting her left arm, Randy showed Brett the marks.

"Intravenous, I'd say."

"It's **ketamine**, fed intravenously," was the answer from crime tech, Mark Johnson, who just walked through the door.

"I just confirmed it. Vets mostly use it. Let me tell you, the dose this lady had, took her on a wild ride."

"What kind of ride?" Brett questioned.

"One that ranks right up there with PCP – nasty."

Brett felt himself **vacillate** between pity and rage. What had this girl ever done to anyone to deserve such a fate? He fantasized how he would **terminate** the killer's life – in ways more painful than what he dealt out.

"That's not all. I found traces of **quinine**. You know? The drug used to treat malaria."

"What the hell?"

Challenge #83

Vacant Stare

MURDER IS ALWAYS PERSONAL. The latest even more so. Detective Brett Connors leaned back in his chair, eyeing his murder board.

The first murder victim was an unidentified Jane Doe who appeared to know her way around the drug scene. She was found in a coffin, the lid off and resting in Mission Bay sand, as if dropped by the sea's **trembling** hand. A carved message of *Die Whore* in the side of the coffin was not the only macabre puzzle piece. The coroner made the grisly discovery that the victim's tongue had been cut out.

Then there was Jane Doe #2– her sightless body dumped on Dr. Maggie Sweeney's balcony. The openings that once held her eyes did little to erase the vacant stare of the dead from Brett's mind. His own narrowed stare defied his body's outward **passivity**. The **tortuous** journey to death of these two Jane Does brought them now to Brett.

Maggie Sweeney – the department's resident shrink and Brett's uncomfortable obsession. Instead of **freaking** out at having a murdered woman dumped on her balcony, the cool lady doc held it together. More than one stressed-out cop challenged that **awesome** control of hers – especially Brett.

Nibbling on a toothpick, a poor substitute for the cigarette he constantly craved, Brett picked up his phone to harass the crime tech, Mark Johnson.

"You got the time, we know the crime," came the **ebullient** voice.

"Cute, Johnson. You ought to have that stitched on a pillow."

"Detective Connors. I didn't know you were into embroidery. I suppose you want to know something more on the vic that went **plonk** on the Doc's door."

"Well, as much as I hate to change the **vivacious** topic, yeah, I'd like to know about the victim – her identity would be a good start."

"No can do, yet, but I'm working on it. There was something else I found out though."

"So, when were you going to tell me?"

"Patience, Detective. I just got the information, no more than five minutes ago. Our little **dynamo** got a piece of this guy."

"You have DNA?" Brett felt his adrenaline punching up.

"Looks like. I need to run it, but do your job and we'll seal the deal."

Challenge #85

The Doctor is In

Brett retrieved the newspaper from the bushes in front of his beach bungalow, cussing another errant toss by the paper boy.

"Kid better forget any dreams of pitching in the majors," he grumbled.

Removing the rubber band from the ever-shrinking paper, Brett laid it on the counter by the brewing coffee. He glanced over at the headline as he poured his first cup of coffee.

BEACH TOWN IS MECCA FOR SERIAL MURDERERS

Brett cussed for the second time that morning as he scanned the story under the sensationalized headline. They made him out to be some damn, **quixotic** avenger of victims as they ran through a list of his solved murders.

Tossing the paper aside, Brett walked to the shower. Maybe he could drown the asinine piece from his mind. He should have known that wouldn't last long. Walking towards his desk, several cops held up the morning's paper.

"Detective, can I have your autograph?"

"I'm sure you'll have this solved by the end of shift, don't you worry."

"Suck my...," his voice trailed off as he saw the lady shrink leaning against his desk.

"Good morning, Detective," the sexy voice seemed to **leap** under his skin with its own fluttering pulse. His gaze latched on the lone **freckle** that kissed her upper lip.

"Doc. You slumming?" he responded, trying for a **vapid** delivery.

"I wondered if you would have time to talk some time today."

"What about?"

"I'd rather discuss it in my office," Maggie said in her controlled, psychiatrist voice, as she looked at her Blackberry calendar. "Would 2:00 work?"

"Schedule all your time in there, Doc," came the **facetious** reply.

Raising her annoyed green gaze, Maggie clipped, "Will 2:00 work, Detective?"

"I'll have to check my calendar. You know, the paper kind."

"Fine," Maggie snapped, "You do that and call my secretary."

There were hoots of laughter as Maggie stormed back to her office. Why did she always **misfire** with Detective Connors? He thought he could **bedazzle** her with his electric, blue stare and very male attitude. Problem was – he could.

Well, she would not **skulk** around him, feeding his massive ego, and offering the soft **coo** of affection he was probably used to from women.

Reaching her office, Maggie took a deep, soothing breath to pull on the professional cloak she wore so well – with everyone but the Detective. Under control, she walked through the door.

"Any messages, **Autumn**?"

And the doctor was in.

Challenge #87

Travesty of Justice

DETECTIVE BRETT CONNORS SAT cooling his heels in the reception area of the precinct's psychiatrist and profiler. He had no doubt it was payback for the hard time he gave her when she was on his turf, asking for a consult.

That he should feel any guilt was a **travesty** of justice, but that's just what he felt – especially with the look the Doc shot his way as she stormed out of the department. One look like that could **eviscerate** the strongest of cops.

"The doctor will see you now," the Cerebus secretary frowned at Brett.

"About damn time," he muttered, trying to keep the **furious** tone to himself. He didn't want to give the lady shrink the satisfaction.

Trying not to **exacerbate** the situation, Brett replaced the scowl on his face with what he hoped was boyish charm – yeah, right.

"So, what did you want to talk about, Doc?"

Maggie held her power position behind her desk as she gestured to one of the two chairs in front of her desk.

"Have a seat, Detective."

"I'll stand if you don't mind."

Forcing a smile, he would not succeed with his own power play, she mused, "I'll strain my neck if I have to keep looking up at you. Please."

"Well, since you asked nice," Brett smirked, easing his 6 foot 4 inch frame into a chair with slender arms no wider than the tip of **antlers** on a young buck. He'd be lucky if it held him – maybe that was her plan – to put him on his ass.

"We are both busy so let me get straight to the point."

"By all means."

"I want in on your investigation."

"Which investigation is that?"

How did this man so easily snap her famous control? She fought hard to mask her **vivacious** nature with the cloak of professionalism, but oh, how the detective tested her.

It was difficult to temper her images of that **squalor** offering of a poor woman laying on her balcony.

"Please, Detective. I thought we agreed not to waste each other's time. I want in on your investigation of the murdered woman, dumped on my doorstep." Her look and tone would **incinerate** a lesser man.

Resisting the urge to make a **bawdy** remark about her use of the word "dump," Brett tried reason instead of his usual protective, **heathen** humor.

"Look, Doc, I know you have more than a passing interest in the case, but you are as much of a victim as that poor girl. I don't think it's a good idea to mix the two."

Challenge #89

Apothecary's Dream

THE MUSTY SMELL WRAPPED invisible fingers of pain around the brightly colored bottles that held an **apothecary**'s dream. Eyes brightened with the madness of remembering the trace of blood the **minx** had left behind. He loved when they struggled.

He mixed a **puree** of nature's evil elixir of the gentle daffodil, the majestic Lily of the Valley, and wrapped it all with the reverent touch of foxglove. So common, so innocuous, yet few knew their deadly kiss of poison. He felt a **shimmer** of anticipation as his eyes moved to his wall of **luscious** victims. He felt the need to **linger** on his ultimate target. How would he play it?

The naked sound of silence awakened to his rasping breath as he grew more and more excited – excited where he'd been and where he had to go. He would show the world. The echoing sound of childhood rants drummed in a relentless beat, “Willy, Willy, **bananas** and nuts, lives in his mother’s house of sluts.”

“Stop it. Shut your face or I’ll cut out your tongue like the whore before you,” he sobbed like the slender, **wand** of a child lost so long ago. There was no **treacle** for the poison of memories burnt in the **wheat** field of forgotten dreams.

-----

treacle: a thick, sticky dark syrup made from partly refined sugar; molasses.

Challenge #91

Got a Hit

In his own form of keyword search, Detective Brett Connors scribbled the words across the lined, yellow tablet with the curling pages.

Jane Doe #1

- *Brunette*
- *5'9"*
- *Slender build*
- *Coffin*
- *Die whore*
- *Drug user*
- *Mission Bay*
- *Tongue cut out*

Jane Doe #2

- *Blonde*
- *5'9"*
- *Slender build*
- *Electrode burns*
- *Drugs in system-user?*
- *Doc's balcony*
- *Eyes cut out*

"You know if you would **reinvest** your paycheck, you could probably get a second-hand laptop."

"You're a real card, McNeill. What do you want?"

"Aren't we the cranky one," his fellow detective, Pat McNeill, responded. "Have another run-in with the lady shrink?"

"McNeill, some of us are working here. So, unless you've got a **sustainable** reason for being here, don't let the door hit you in the ass."

“You don’t have a door. Okay, okay,” he said, raising his hands in surrender at Brett’s curled lip. Tossing a folder on Brett’s desk, Pat remarked, “I think this will give me a **preemptive** pass to your undying gratitude.”

Moving the folder off his **badge** that lay on top of his desk, Brett flipped open the folder.

“We got a hit on the DNA.”

“Our killer finally made a mistake.”

“Well, maybe, maybe not.”

“What the hell does that mean? Are you purposely trying to **obfuscate** this discussion or does it just come naturally?”

“Obfuscate? Have you been reading again? I told you that was dangerous for your health. Okay, shit, you used to have a sense of humor. We got a hit on the DNA, but here’s the thing. It’s some dead guy’s.”

“Someone they just brought in?”

“No, someone who’s been dead for five years.”

“Have you been hitting the **bourbon** again, McNeill?”

"That is an **unsubstantiated** rumor. I would never **relinquish** my love affair with the King of **Kings'** Beer for rot-gut whiskey. The rumor holds absolutely no **credence**."

Fuck you, McNeill."

"I'll pass."

Challenge #93

Dined Alone

"SOON THEY WILL **UNDERSTAND**," the killer silently spoke to one no longer there.

He was tired of all the **rhetoric** in the news. Couldn't they come up with something more creative than the "torturer of women"? Journalism was not what it used to be. So-called writers would **embalm** words in placid replication, whipping the public with the senseless **flagellation** of mediocrity.

"There is no sense of pride in one's work, Robert," he muttered.

"I'm sorry, did you say something?"

Frustrated at the interruption, he calmed himself as Robert offered a soothing response in his ear.

"No, I'm fine, thank you."

"Did you want another margarita or more **guacamole**?"

Battling for control, he wrapped his hand around the **bougainvillea**, surrounding the outside patio. Crushing it, he imagined it to be the skinny neck of the unattractive, annoying waitress. She was not worthy of his **passion.**

"I'm fine. Just bring me the check please."

"We should have dined at home with the fine bottle of pinot **noir**, Robert," he mumbled, tracing the **stigmata** wounds left by the sharp thorns of the bougainvillea, "instead of enduring the **impudent** behavior of someone so beneath us."

Flicking his coat in disgust, he rose – the incident soon forgotten.

The waitress tracked his exit with a cautious look at the man who had dined alone.

"Freakin' nut case."

Challenge #95

Timewarp of Madness

SLAMMING THE **METAL** BARS of the cage, the killer planned his final journey. He laid out the **eclectic** collection of torture and vowed he would not **renege** on his promise.

In a **timewarp** of madness, he was transported to another time. He played the **puppet** as a **toddler** until the time where he took the strands. He felt it was his right, his destiny, and not a **misappropriated** piece of time. But, then did the mad really understand?

He ran the blade over the **leather** strap, over and over, with the precision of a perfected task. No matter how **guarded**, the killer knew, his final victim would know the **nightmare** that was his past.

Challenge #97

Journey of Another Time

DETECTIVE BRETT CONNORS WASN'T a fan of the holidays. Nana Connors, his only family, in the truest sense of the word, had been gone a few years now. Yet, for some reason, he was **uncharacteristically** happy this year. He didn't even mind that he was in a mall, just weeks before Christmas.

He smiled as he watched antsy kids, tugging on their Mom's hands, as they rushed to get in line to see Santa. He passed a table where a young girl, her tongue caught between her teeth, was carefully creating Christmas **origami** designs. She had a snowflake, holly and a really cute **penguin**.

"Hey, those are really good."

Blue eyes sparkled like twinkling lights on a Christmas tree as dimpled smile reached out and grabbed his heart.

"Thank you, sir. Want to try it?

He might as well write a book on **Egyptology**.

“Thanks, sweetheart, but I’d rather buy one from an expert. How much are they?”

“Oh, they don’t cost anything. I just like to share them. Which one do you want?”

When’s the last time you heard a kid at Christmas giving away the chance of getting some money?

“I’ll take the blue star. It’ll remind me of your pretty blue eyes.”

She giggled as she felt her heart **balloon** with her first crush. Brett would have laughed, had he known. He thought he was more likely to be thought of as the scary **ogre**, a product of a child's worst nightmare

“Merry Christmas.”

“It is now.” Brett bent over and gave the innocent cheek a kiss of thanks, “Merry Christmas, sweetheart.”

Brett meandered along the mall. Stopping in front of the display at the bookstore, Brett looked at a copy of Charles Dickens’ David Copperfield, a great example of the **bildungsroman** style Brett loved as a child.

The mall was decked out in all its **aesthetically** pleasing glitter, and Brett sighed with the memory of how much Nana's eyes would brighten at Christmas time. He could almost smell the cookies cooling on their racks. She could have made a fortune on a **franchise** of those cookies. But, then she didn't need the money.

"Merry Christmas, Nana. I love you," Brett whispered.

He turned to walk down the **slope** into the food court. The cold, hard stare of evil damned him as he strolled along on his journey of another time.

Bildungsroman: a novel dealing with one person's formative years or spiritual education.

Challenge #100

The Swagger

As Brett chowed down on his Food Court pizza, he wondered if the Lady Doc would consider his gift too **extravagant**. He wasn't even sure why he bought the district's shrink and profiler a gift.

The 1998 Clos des Goisses Brut **champagne** went for $250 a bottle. For most cops, calling the gift extravagant was an understatement. Thanks to a very generous inheritance from Nana Connors, Brett didn't need to worry about money. Yet he still worked some of the most gruesome murders in the state. After 25 years as a homicide detective, Brett Connors didn't know any other way. He simply **accepted** it as his life.

As if his thoughts conjured her up, Brett straightened in his chair, like a recalcitrant schoolboy, at the sight of the long-legged, Dr. Margaret Mary Sweeney across the mall. He silently cursed himself for the **lasting** effect the lady shrink had on him. She was trouble with a capital T.

He watched as a guy with **unmitigated** gall wrapped his arms around Maggie, lifting her off the floor in a huge embrace. Her face glowed with the joy of the season as she laughed and kissed the guy – on the lips, no less.

Brett watched as she grabbed the guy's hand and dragged him over to an empty table. Removing her winter coat to reveal form-hugging jeans, Brett softly whistled between his teeth in admiration. **Who knew** what she had under that clinical white coat she always wore?

Deciding he had enough of this guy, Brett tossed the remains of his pizza, and took his 6 foot 4 inch frame over to their table.

"Hey, Doc, fancy meeting you here."

Brett watched as the smile faded from Maggie's lips and her green forest eyes blinked in surprise.

"Detective Connors, hello."

"Aren't you going to introduce me to your friend?" Brett all but sneered.

Maggie, uncharacteristically flustered, replied, "Oh, I'm sorry. This is my friend, Shane Arthur. Shane, this is Detective Brett Connors"

"Hey, buddy, nice to meet you. Why don't you join us?"

Brett eased his tall body into the Food Court comedy for chairs and wondered if this guy was the **yardstick** the Doc used for what she found attractive.

"So, how do you know the Doc?"

"Oh, Maggie and I go way back. I guess you could say we met in a **plethora** of words," he laughed, sharing a much too intimate glance with the Doc – at least to Brett's way of thinking.

"Shane is an editing genius and the creator of the hot site, Creative Copy Challenge. Maybe you heard of it?" Maggie smiled with an affectionate touch to Shane's arm that had Brett's eyes narrowing into blue ice chips of disdain.

"Never heard of it," Brett grumbled.

"Maggie tends to exaggerate. It's one of the reasons I love her so much. Look I promised the kids we would hit Sea World early. It was so good seeing you, Maggie."

Brett watched the two exchange another hug and kiss. Kids? Married? Divorced?

"I am so glad I met you, Detective. Maggie has told me so much about you."

Brett's startled look caught Maggie's quick blush.

"I hope to see you two again real soon. Happy holidays!"

Brett watched the **swagger** of a confident man as he walked away.

"Well, I **hope** you know that if it wasn't for Shane, you wouldn't even exist," Maggie fumed, snapping her coat from the chair; she grabbed her belongings and stormed off in disgust.

"Now, what the hell does that mean?" Brett mused.

Challenge #106

Feigned Disinterest

BRETT CONNORS WASN'T SURE if he was glad the holidays were over. On the one hand, the precinct had been as quiet as Randy Watkin's workplace. Randy was the city's coroner. On the other hand, Brett was glad his fellow detective, Pat McNeill, was back from vacation. Now, maybe they could get back to the little things, like finding a serial killer.

Pat walked in with his hands shoved into his windbreaker's pouch, looking like some kind of baby-carrying **marsupial**.

"I thought it never rained in southern California."

"We bring in rain as a **delusion** tactic for tourists."

"Yeah, well I find it pretty damn delusional."

"That's because you're from the east coast."

"And you are such a gnarly dude, Connors."

Brett chuckled at the detective's scowl. After 25 years of homicide, Brett was relieved he could still find the humor in life.

"Grab some coffee and let's take a look at the coroner's reports on our psycho," Brett instructed while pulling together the **corresponding** files. This case had been going on so long he was surprised the pages had not turned **yellow**.

"I'm not sure what **purpose** it'll serve. I swear we have gone over them until our eyes bled."

"He's still out there, even though we have DNA, so we are obviously missing something."

"We have the DNA of a dead guy. So, unless he came back from the grave, how can he be our psycho killer?"

Good question, Brett thought. They thought they finally had a break in the case when the coroner made the **grand** announcement that the last victim had DNA under her fingernails. After months of investigation, the elation they **justly** felt, deflated like a New Year's balloon in March.

Brett's hatred of this sick motherfucker took on **xenophobic** proportions. The killer left one victim without a tongue and the other with no eyes. And that was just, pardon the pun, the visual of his sick torture. Then he made it personal by dumping the last victim on Dr. Maggie Sweeney's balcony.

Brett had long ago **recanted** his feigned disinterest in the precinct's sexy psychiatrist and profiler. In fact, the long-legged, green-eyed seductress had **spoiled** him for his typical type.

"Hello, Brett, anyone home?"

Brett blinked in surprise at the sound of his fellow detective. Obviously, he had been trying to get Brett's attention for some time.

"Just thinking about the case."

"Yeah, right, and I get all moon-eyed over the motherfucker killer, too."

----

xenophobic: fear or hatred of strangers

Challenge #111

Highway to Nowhere

THIS WINTER WAS ONE **mudslide** after another. And now it was really cold – okay, cold for San Diego. Wrapped in her warm, fuzzy coat, Maggie felt like a bad imitation of an **Ewok**, puffed up from **lactose intolerance**.

As she began to **creep** down Interstate 5 towards work, she hoped San Diego could **kiss the rain** good-bye. It had been an unusually rainy winter.

"So spoiled," she smiled to herself.

Maggie's thoughts drifted to her day ahead as the Encinitas police district psychiatrist and profiler. Capturing a serial killer had become the district's obsession. The district **funnel**ed almost all its resources into finding the killer and his capture had become very personal – to Maggie and Detective Brett Connors.

Maggie wondered if her **pusillanimous** behavior stemmed more from having the killer dump a body on her balcony or from the threat of the very sexy detective getting past her defenses.

Okay, she wasn't going down that path. Shaking off an anxious feeling, Maggie glanced at the clock. She had a 9 a.m. meeting with a colleague from **Larkspur** (in northern California) and she had some last-minute research she wanted to finish.

It was an interesting case, except for its victims. A serial killer in the small community had a very disturbing calling card. He, or perhaps more likely she, would **castrate** victims before dumping them alongside a deserted road.

"Come on, **Poplolly**," she coaxed, using her nickname for her 1985 VW Bug, "let's get off this highway to nowhere."

With her mind on the meeting, Maggie didn't notice the dark sedan following her down the frontage road.

----

pusillanimous: showing a lack of courage or determination; timid.

Challenge #113

The Hunter

HE FLEW **UNDER** HER radar and she did not remember. Soon she would be singing with **angels** as the devil inside triumphed once more. He watched, though she did not see, as she entered the **code** into the door. It did not matter. He memorized the code.

His rage built through the **tunnels** of his mind as he knew he was an **incognito** form unrecognized by her and all the rest. This wasn't about a **quota**. This was revenge, in its purest form. The rest meant nothing. But, she was different. She would regret how she kicked him to the curb like a recalcitrant **dog**.

His felt the memories **war** with his need to suppress them. They pounded at him like a nagging **wife**, in a kaleidoscope **puzzle** that was his life. He fought for control, as he once more became the hunter.

***

Detective Connors walked past the precinct's front desk, greeting Angie, the volunteer receptionist.

"Detective Connors, have you seen Dr. Sweeney?"

Refraining from uttering the sarcastic response that rose to mind, the detective merely replied, "No, why?"

"She had an appointment with the profiler from Larkspur half an hour ago and she hasn't shown up. That's not like Dr. Sweeney.

No, it wasn't – at all.

Creative Copy for the Soul

DID YOU MAKE UP stories as a child? Was an imaginary friend your confidant? Or did you battle the bad guys through video games or your favorite book series?

Being the middle child of seven and born long before most of you, imagination sparked my childhood play. Nancy Drew books took my imagination by the hand and opened the door to the magic of words. It has taken me a long time to make my own words the center of who I am.

Taking a huge leap by leaving the corporate world behind, I began freelancing as a professional business writer. I gave myself permission to make writing my business. But like so many business writers, my personal writing goals were placed on the backburner. Client projects always came first. Or maybe that was an excuse.

When I finally retired from business writing, I had no more excuses. Sure there are challenges. We all have them. But slowly that permission to write extended to my personal writing. I am so thankful I discovered Creative Copy Challenge (CCC) during my business writing days. While I was busy earning a living, CCC allowed me to keep the flame burning of what could be. It was creative copy for my soul.

Now It's Your Turn

Even if you are not a writer or have no interest in becoming one, word prompt challenges center your thoughts. The challenges wake up the sleeping child who invented stories with no thought of criticism or judgment. The best play was the one you created yourself. So, give it a try. No AI. No criticism. No judgment. Just you and your words. Magical.

No Rules

THE FIRST RULE ABOUT using word prompts: #1 – There are no rules.

The following is Creative Copy Challenge's instructions the site used as a guide.

Writing Prompts – Creative Copy Challenge

Here are 10 words. They are semi-related... and sometimes not. That's what makes it a challenge...take these 10 words...and see how you can use them in a poem, a piece of flash fiction, a short short story...
You never know when being relaxed about your writing can help you focus on your main project or... just come here each week, play with words, help your children have fun with words and challenge them to write too.

The short stories I shared in this book relate to the Death and the Detective series I developed at CCC. Other participants also wrote series. Kenn Crawford, wrote a hilarious series, *The Saga of Bayou Billy*, that he later published.

My good friend, Mitch Allen, converted this non-lover of science fiction or fantasy with his wildly imaginative CCC series. You can find his CCC-inspired entries sprinkled throughout his site, Morpho Designs. https://morphodesigns.com/And another CCC alumni who published his fantasy series (and a lot more) at his site is Aaron Pogue.

Short stories or series are but one example of how to use the word prompts. I have multiple entries that took a different approach and were not related to the detective series. For most of my entries, I would challenge myself further by using the word prompts in the order in which they were listed. My other CCC colleagues scattered them throughout their creative copy in no particular order. Again, that is the beauty of word prompts – no rules.

Although Creative Copy Challenge is no longer active with new word prompts, you can still access the site (as of this writing) and choose to use any of the word prompts provided there. The current url is: https://creativecopychallenge.wordpress.com/

Countless sites offer word prompts. The following are a few of those sites (I have no affiliation with them). Of course, you can also create your own list of word prompts. Remember – no rules.

Writer's Digest Creative Writing Prompts (https://www.writersdigest.com/prompts)

Poet & Writers Writing Prompts & Exercises (https://www.pw.org/writing-prompts-exercises)

Reedsy Weekly Writing Prompts (https://reedsy.com/creative-writing-prompts/)

Writing Exercises Creative Writing Prompts (https://writingexercises.co.uk/)

Think Written 365 Creative Writing Prompts (https://thinkwritten.com/365-creative-writing-prompts/)

If you would like to take a shot with the word prompts used in my Death and the Detective series, I have included a list of each challenge's word prompts at the end of this book. Go ahead. Write a better detective series – or whatever your little heart desires.

Walking a better path for connecting to yourself and the world we live in.

Word Prompts List

Death and the Detective

Challenge #1

1. X-Factor

2. Townhall

3. Parrot

4. Cracker Jacks

5. Unions

6. Google

7. Napkins

8. The 10 Commandments

9. San Francisco

10. Cold Season

Challenge #2

1. Winnie the Pooh
2. Prior work history
3. Bathroom
4. Song
5. Head-shot
6. Authorities
7. Lawsuits
8. Propaganda
9. Twitter
10. Orange Juice

Challenge #3

1. Sawubona – sah-wu-bo-na (Zulu for I see you. I recognize you as a worthy person in front of me.)

2. Nothing to lose
3. Discover
4. Concrete
5. Yoga
6. After Hours
7. Home Alone
8. Landslide
9. Library
10. Nap Time

Challenge #4

1. Time Will Tell
2. Experience Preferred
3. Plywood
4. Poet
5. Gold Rush

6. Scenario

7. Influx

8. Winter

9. Velvet

10. Road Block

Challenge #5

1. Search

2. Danger Zone

3. Sun Rays

4. Gunslinger

5. Armor

6. Astronaut

7. Poodle

8. Retaliation

9. Limousine

10. Journalism

Challenge #8

1. One thing leads to another

2. Ruffian

3. Extrovert

4. Tranquility

5. Unlimited Access

6. Lantern

7. Dishwasher

8. Coffin

9. Barrier

10. Between the lines

Challenge #9

1. Daydreamer

2. Silkworms

3. Painkillers
4. You got lucky
5. Catcall
6. Phobia
7. Iron-ore
8. Wavelength
9. Closed fist
10. Desire

Challenge #10

1. Bubble wrap
2. Sick Fucker
3. Gumdrop
4. Culmination
5. Horseback
6. Ammonia

7. Little by little

8. Irregular

9. Scapegoat

10. Birdcage

Challenge #11

1. Stupidity

2. Deathtrap

3. In the name of love

4. Switchblade

5. Gunpowder

6. Clobber

7. Kindergarten

8. Sorrow

9. Goatee

10. Asylum

Challenge #13

1. Coke
2. Glacier
3. Cesspool
4. Womanizer
5. Rancid
6. Paycheck
7. Imposter
8. Tablet
9. Just an illusion
10. Shield

Challenge #14

1. Shadow
2. Trespass
3. Warmth

4. Fragrant
5. Doppelganger
6. Cupid
7. Butterfly effect
8. Luminescent
9. Velvet
10. Simpatico

Challenge #15

1. Eyes of a stranger
2. Gumbo
3. Contraband
4. Meadow
5. Shimmer
6. Nude
7. Fall on me

8. Dolphin

9. Sidestep

10. Death

Challenge #17

1. Red wine

2. Hurricane

3. Scary Monsters

4. Photograph

5. Drama

6. Prophylactic

7. Morgue

8. Hysterical

9. Wheelchair

10. Stain

Challenge #18

1. Do you hear me?
2. Gut
3. Evil
4. Felony
5. Revolution
6. Riptide
7. It's hard
8. Vagrant
9. Lush
10. Lightning

Challenge #19

1. If I could turn back time
2. Slaughter
3. Residue

4. Lunacy
5. Tyrant
6. Luxury
7. Foreigner
8. Cocaine
9. Broken
10. Sniper

Challenge #21

1. Totally 80s
2. Miracle
3. Dinosaur
4. Tattoo
5. Shrinkage
6. Reversible
7. Poison

8. Wheelbarrow

9. Epoxy

10. Dreamland

Challenge #22

1. Don't turn around

2. Rage

3. Candy

4. Play

5. Recap

6. Mischief

7. Tabloid

8. Don't tell me

9. Harp

10. Crackpot

Challenge #23

1. Half way there

2. Primitive

3. Spacesuit

4. All night long

5. Waitress

6. Dropout

7. Medallion

8. Relax

9. Tranquilizer

10. Solitude

Challenge #25

1. You want it? You got it!
2. Ransom
3. Mania
4. It's gone
5. Nanosecond
6. Coward
7. Throttle
8. Lemonade
9. Vault
10. Robot

Challenge #27

1. Fascination
2. Stance
3. Patience

4. Cult
5. Propose
6. Wolf
7. Be yourself
8. Police
9. Seagull
10. Knock me down

Challenge #29

1. Midnight
2. Divine
3. Voices
4. Charm
5. Sensation
6. Yes
7. Departure

8. Domino

9. Canary

10. Camera

Challenge #30

1. Rain

2. What have I done?

3. Triangle

4. Change your mind

5. Out of order

6. Heart

7. Missile

8. Fantastic

9. Atomic

10. Picture

Challenge #31

1. Scout
2. Never stop
3. So far so good
4. Hair
5. Digital
6. Stink
7. Unavoidable
8. Lyrics
9. Pulse
10. Infection

Challenge #33

1. If you leave
2. Future
3. A place to hide

4. Fate
5. Ride
6. Avalanche
7. Do without
8. In the dark
9. Break Away
10. View

Challenge #35

1. One in a million
2. Pretend
3. Night
4. Load
5. Fable
6. With or without
7. Victim

8. Squeeze
9. Nylon
10. Crowd

Challenge #37

1. When I grow up
2. Just one thing
3. Flirt
4. Sign
5. Slippery
6. So far away
7. The end
8. Spice
9. Wrong
10. Fear

Challenge #39

1. Terror
2. No problem
3. A little closer
4. Casual
5. Float
6. Respond
7. Release
8. Forever
9. Line
10. Doubt

Challenge #41

1. Do you know?
2. Push
3. Something more

4. Quest
5. Phony
6. Perfect
7. Remember
8. Devil
9. Scene
10. Waste

Challenge #43

1. Hero
2. Smoke
3. Idiot
4. Ponder
5. Fortune
6. Reflection
7. Jump

8. Used to be
9. Settle down
10. Round

Challenge #46

1. Shirt
2. Gather
3. Race
4. Compulsive
5. Burn
6. Star
7. Nonsense
8. Temper
9. Think about it
10. Sharp

Challenge #48

1. Seize

2. Swig

3. Dawn

4. Popular

5. Clear

6. Sour

7. Gain

8. Part

9. Fake

10. Overcome

Challenge #50

1. Press

2. Lucky

3. Turn

4. Provocative
5. Giddy
6. Against
7. Cozy
8. Flatter
9. Tender
10. Top

Challenge #52

1. All too well
2. React
3. Fill
4. Divert
5. Jolt
6. Cheer
7. Curse

8. Ache

9. Club

10. Embrace

Challenge #54

1. Random

2. Shatter

3. Apart

4. Answer

5. Rhyme

6. Figure

7. Pass

8. Blank

9. Ignore

10. Explain

Challenge #56

1. Big shot
2. Smash
3. Whole
4. Move
5. Force
6. Write
7. Sure
8. Prove
9. Sense
10. Unusual

Challenge #58

1. Guilty
2. Distract
3. Astronomical

4. Tremble
5. Wrestling
6. Elephant
7. Portal
8. League
9. Larynx
10. Magic

Challenge #59

1. Tomorrow
2. Smooth
3. Automated
4. Legend
5. Master
6. Better
7. Narrow

8. Hard
9. Size
10. Combination

Challenge #61

1. Fancy
2. Razor
3. Attack
4. Neglect
5. Fool
6. Nimble
7. Wired
8. Shift
9. Squeamish
10. Threat

Challenge #63

1. Abduct
2. Addictive
3. Captive

4. Detail

5. Mimic

6. Motive

7. Pattern

8. Return

9. Steady

10. Sturdy

Challenge #65

1. Clue

2. Dance

3. Dial

4. Divide

5. Fog

6. Lonely

7. Recall

8. Reminder
9. Rough
10. Torch

Challenge #67

1. Agony
2. Double
3. Frozen
4. Instant
5. Motion
6. Oval
7. Royal
8. Rule
9. Sorry
10. Track

Challenge #69

1. Anxious
2. Chain
3. Coercive
4. Conventional
5. Current
6. Disposition
7. Dynamic
8. Inward
9. Social
10. Stalk

Challenge #71

1. Alive
2. Dust
3. Gloom

4. Mad
5. Mirage
6. Piece
7. Sleep
8. Tackle
9. Tendency
10. Welcome

Challenge #73

1. Thud
2. Pop
3. Pendulum
4. Linoleum
5. Fond
6. Hysteric
7. Smidgen

8. Giggle
9. Intonation
10. Retrospect

Challenge #75

1. Sleepy
2. Ascend
3. Acidic
4. Sugar
5. Retain
6. Contract
7. Outdated
8. Comment
9. Estimate
10. Original

Challenge #77

1. Crawl
2. If that's what it takes
3. Wait
4. Bring
5. Wrinkle
6. Junk
7. Total
8. Emerge
9. Steep
10. Anything

Challenge #79

1. Wash
2. Sticky
3. Soft

4. Instead

5. Tube

6. Castle

7. Bundle

8. Stone

9. Challenge

10. Notice

Challenge #81

1. Corpulent

2. Furrow

3. Don

4. Dowager

5. Opulent

6. Resplendent

7. Ketamine

8. Vacillate
9. Terminate
10. Quinine

Challenge #83

1. Trembling
2. Passivity
3. Torturous
4. Freaking
5. Awesome
6. Nibbling
7. Ebullient
8. Plonk – Cheap or inferior wine; to drop or be dropped heavily or suddenly
9. Vivacious
10. Dynamo

Challenge #85

1. Quixotic – impulsive; Caught up in the romance of noble deeds and the pursuit of unreachable goals
2. Leap
3. Freckle
4. Vapid
5. Facetious
6. Misfire
7. bedazzle
8. Skulk
9. Coo – To talk fondly or amorously in murmurs
10. Autumn

Challenge #87

1. Travesty
2. Eviscerate

3. Furious
4. Exacerbate
5. Antlers
6. Vivacious
7. Squalor
8. Incinerate
9. Bawdy
10. Heathen

Challenge #89

1. Apothecary
2. Minx
3. Puree
4. Shimmer
5. Luscious
6. Linger

7. Bananas

8. Wand

9. Treacle – British Molasses; A medicinal compound formerly used as an antidote for poison; anything sweet and cloying

10. Wheat OR motherf#cker

Challenge #91

1. Reinvest

2. Sustainable

3. Preemptive

4. Badge

5. Obfuscate – To make so confused as to be difficult to understand

6. Bourbon

7. Unsubstantiated

8. Relinquish

9. Kings

10. Credence

Challenge #93

1. Understand
2. Rhetoric
3. Embalm
4. Flagellation
5. Guacamole
6. Bougainvillea
7. Passion
8. Noir – Of or relating to a genre of crime literature
9. Stigmata – marks resembling the wounds on the crucified body of Christ
10. Impudentt

Challenge #95

1. Metal

2. Eclectic
3. Renege
4. Timewarp
5. Puppet
6. Toddler
7. Mispppropriated
8. Leather
9. Guarded
10. Nightmare

Challenge #97

1. Uncharacteristically
2. Origami
3. Penguin
4. Egyptology
5. Balloon

6. Ogre

7. Bildungsroman – A genre of books in which the protagonist develops both morally and psychologically throughout childhood and into adulthood.

8. Aesthetically

9. Franchise

10. Slope

Challenge #100

1. Extravagant

2. Champagne

3. Accepted

4. Lasting

5. Unmitigated – not diminished in intensity, severity; (intensifier) an unmitigated disaster

6. Who knew

7. Yardstick

8. Plethora – an excess; An excess of blood in the circulatory system or in one organ or area.

9. Swagger - strut, brag, or boastful; to bully

10. Hope

Challenge #106

1. Marsupial – kangaroos, opossums, bandicoots, and wombats, found principally in Australia and the Americas.

2. Delusion

3. Corresponding

4. Yellow

5. Purpose

6. Grand

7. Justly

8. Xenophobic – unduly fearful of that which is foreign, especially of strangers or foreign peoples

9. Recanted

10. Spoiled

Challenge #111

1. Mudslide
2. Ewok
3. Lactose intolerance
4. Creep
5. Kiss the Rain
6. Funnel
7. Pusillanimous – characterized by a lack of courage or determination
8. Larkspur – plants of the genus Delphinium, with spikes of blue, pink, or white irregular spurred flowers
9. Castrate
10. Poplolly – an affectionate term, little darling

Challenge #113

1. Under
2. Angels
3. Code
4. Tunnels
5. Incognito
6. Quota
7. Dog
8. War
9. Wife
10. Puzzle

www.ingramcontent.com/pod-product-compliance
Lightning Source LLC
LaVergne TN
LVHW020713110826
845149LV00012B/2237

* 9 7 9 8 9 9 3 3 5 2 9 3 0 *